Night-time Tale

for Klaus

Published by Hinkler Books Pty Ltd
45–55 Fairchild Street
Heatherton Victoria 3202 Australia
www.hinkler.com.au

hinkler

First published by Andersen Press Ltd., London

Text © Ruth Brown 2005
Illustrations © Ruth Brown 2005
Cover design © Hinkler Books 2011

Cover design: Peter Tovey
Prepress: Graphic Print Group

ISBN: 978 1 7435 2446 6

Printed and bound in China

Night~time Tale

by Ruth Brown

hinkler

"Are you awake, Mama? I had a bad dream.
It frightened me so, I can't sleep, Mama.

I was in a dark forest and there was a house . . .

. . . a house made of candy and gingerbread.

I tasted a piece — but an old witch jumped out.
She frightened me so I just ran, Mama.

I ran very fast and bumped into a girl,
a girl who was going to her grandma's.

We went to the house where her gran was in bed.

She smiled at us both, but her teeth were SO big . . .

... and her hands and her face were hairy and grey.
She frightened me so I just ran, Mama.

I ran and I ran, then I stopped and looked up —
I saw a great beanstalk that reached to the sky.

A giant slid down and crashed to the ground.
He left a huge hole where he landed.

I went to the edge to see where he'd gone
and felt somebody PUSH me, right over.

I fell down and down then woke with a bump.
Can I come in with you? I can't sleep, Mama."

"There, there," Mama said, "there's no need to fear.
They're just fairytales, they can't hurt you . . .

Come in with me and go back to sleep —
You'll be tired as can be in the morning."

So Baby Bear climbed into Mama Bear's bed . . .

. . . and soon they were peacefully sleeping.